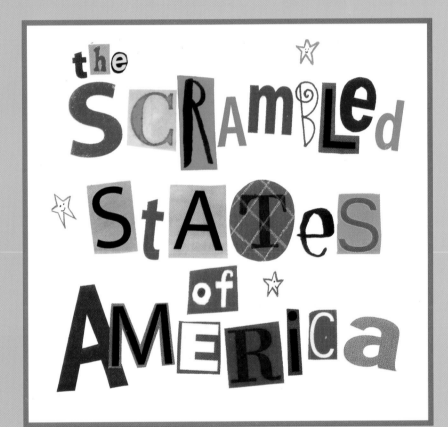

the Scrambled States of America

way
up
there

Alaska

Canada

C A

Washington

Mont

OREGON

Idaho

W

California

Nevada

Utah

Pacific Ocean

Arizona

way
down
there

Hawaii

M E

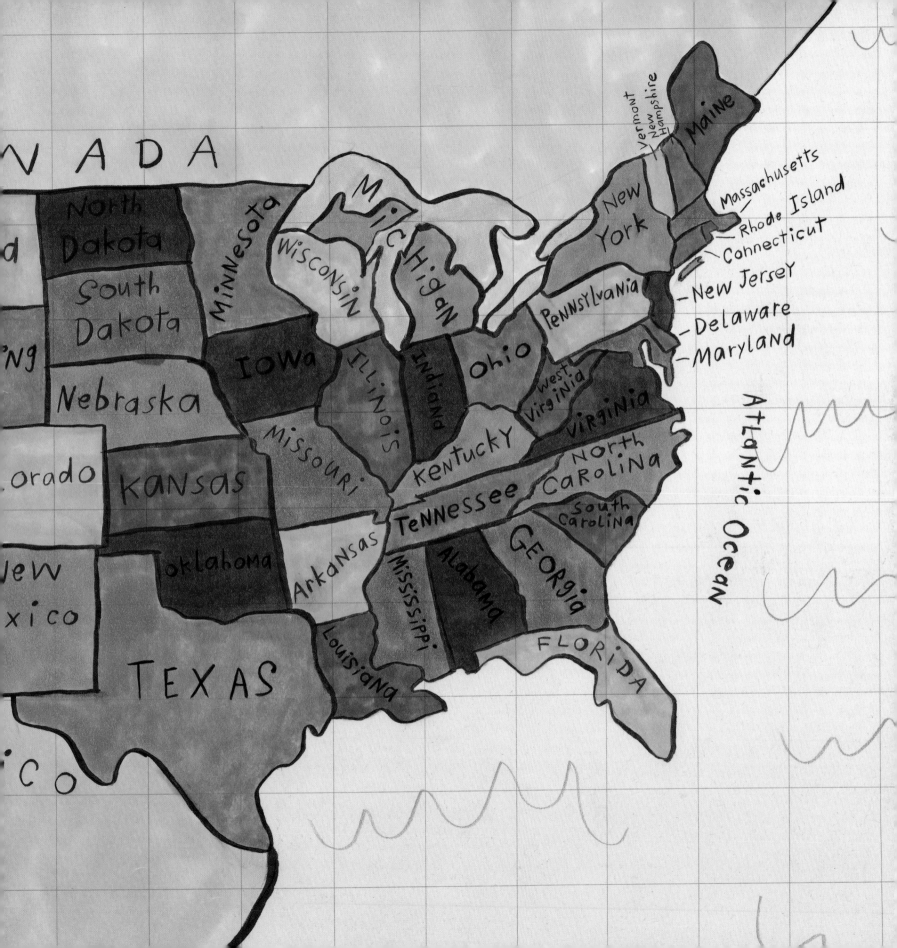

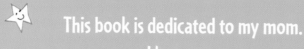

This book is dedicated to my mom.
I love you.
–Laurie

TH IS BOOK BELONGS TO:

_ _

WHO LIVES IN THE STATE OF:

_ _

A thank-you song to Christy: More than an editor, More than an editor to meeee.
(To be sung to a Bee Gees tune)

Henry Holt and Company, LLC, *Publishers since 1866*, 175 Fifth Avenue, New York, New York 10010
www.HenryHoltKids.com

Henry Holt® is a registered trademark of Henry Holt and Company, LLC.
Copyright © 1998 by Laurie Keller. All rights reserved.
Distributed in Canada by H.B. Fenn and Company Ltd.

Library of Congress Cataloging-in-Publication Data
Keller, Laurie. The scrambled states of America / Laurie Keller.
Summary: The states become bored with their positions on the map and decide
to change places for a while. Also includes facts about the states.
1. U.S. states—Juvenile Fiction. [1. United States—Fiction.] I. Title.
PZ7.K281346Sc 1998 [E]–dc21 97-50418

ISBN-13: 978-0-8050-5802-4 / ISBN-10: 0-8050-5802-8 (hardcover)
18 20 22 24 25 23 21 19
ISBN-13: 978-0-8050-6831-3 / ISBN-10: 0-8050-6831-7 (paperback)
12 14 16 18 20 22 24 25 23 21 19 17 15 13

First published in hardcover in 1998 by Henry Holt and Company.
First paperback edition, 2002

Designed by Meredith Baldwin
Printed in China on acid-free paper. ∞
The artist used acrylic paint, colored pencils, marker, and collage
on illustration board to create the illustrations for this book.
Factual information about the states on pages 32 to 35 is from
The Doubleday Atlas of the United States of America, by Josephine Bacon (New York: Doubleday, 1990).

the SCRAMBLED STATES of AMERICA

By LAURIE KELLER

HENRY HOLT AND COMPANY
New York

HI THERE.

I'm Sam. I'm assuming since you opened this book that you're in the mood to hear a story. Well, you're in luck, because I have a story for you. It's a little story about this fine country of ours. I'll bet you thought you'd heard 'em all, but not many people know this one.

Hi, I'M New Jersey. I'M Not new and I'm not wearing a jersey. Go figure!

Do you MiND?!

Idaho

Hi. I'm a star. A star with a hat.

Let ME tell it!

Oh, oh, let ME! Let ME!

OHIO

COLORADO

No, no, you two— that part is my job. Now get back in your places. We're about to start the story.

OREGON

TEXAS
MMMM

Aren't they cute?

Let's give them a couple of seconds to get back into position. One thousand ONE. One thousand TWO. One thousand THREE.

OK, turn the page!

*! © # I could've told it!...

Well, it was just your basic, ordinary day in the good old U.S. of A.
States all over the country were waking up, having their first
cups of coffee, reading the morning paper, and enjoying
the beautiful sunrise.

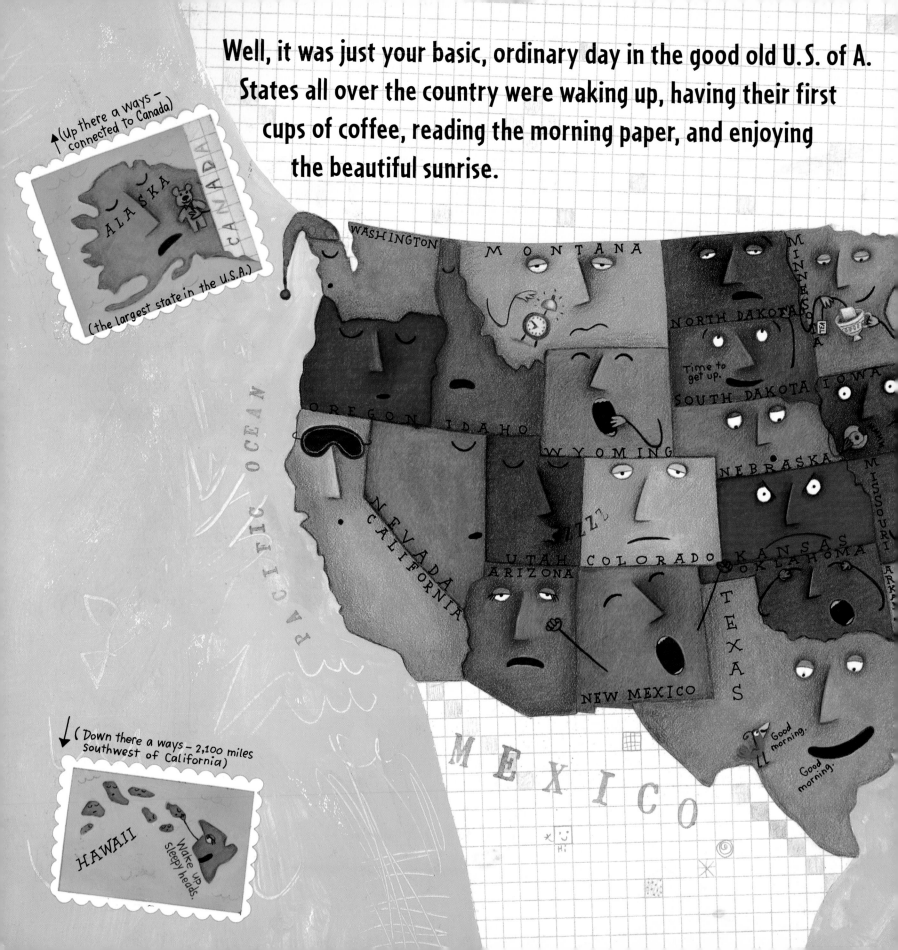

↑ (Up there a ways —
connected to Canada)

(the largest state in the U.S.A.)

↓ (Down there a ways — 2,100 miles
southwest of California)

All the states, that is,
except for Kansas.

He was not feeling happy at all.

How do I know this?
Because he said,

I'M NOT FEELING HAPPY AT ALL!

Close-up of KANSAS

"What's wrong?"
his best friend, Nebraska, kindly asked him.
(Nebraska is a very kind state.)

"I don't know," moaned Kansas. "I just feel bored. All day long we just sit here in the middle of the country. We never **GO** anywhere. We never **DO** anything, and we <u>**NEVER**</u> meet any **NEW** states!"

"Hmmmmm . . ." said Nebraska.

"Don't get me wrong, Nebraska. You're the best friend a state could have.

But don't you ever want more? Don't you ever want to see what else is out there?"

Nebraska's thought process →

"Yes! Yes, I do!" Nebraska said excitedly. "And now that you mention it, I'm sick and tired of hearing North Dakota and South Dakota bicker all the time!"

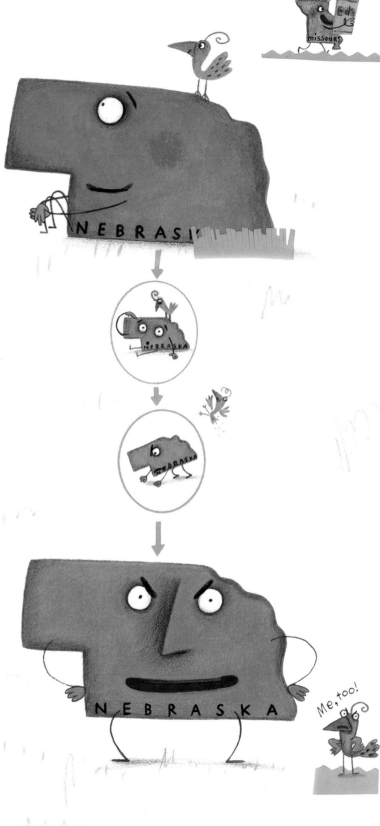

Me, too!

I HAVE A GREAT IDEA!

exclaimed Kansas.

Kansas
Scale of Miles
0 10 20 30 40 50
N

(WOW! His smile is 285 miles wide!)

"Let's have a party and invite all the other states! You know, one of those get-to-know-you deals. Everyone can bring a favorite dish. We could have music and dancing. . . ."

"That's a GREAT idea!"
shrieked Nebraska.
"I wish I'd thought of it myself."

So, with a little help from their neighbors, Missouri and Iowa,
those wacky little midwestern states planned the biggest party ever.

They sent out invitations,

and blew up balloons.

They even hired a band to play.

At last, the big day came, and little by little the states arrived at the party. Nebraska and Kansas were on the welcoming committee, Iowa was in charge of coats, and Missouri and Illinois passed out name tags for each state to wear.

Within minutes after their arrival, the states began making friends with each other. They spent hours talking, laughing, dancing, and singing.

It was long into the evening when Idaho and Virginia got up on the stage.

"Excuse me," Idaho said politely. (Idaho is a very polite state.) "Sorry to interrupt, but Virginia and I were just talking and we thought it might be fun if she and I switched places—you know—so we could see a new part of the country."

"Yes," Virginia chimed in. "Then we thought maybe all of you might want to try it, too. What do you think?"

A wave of excitement swept through the room.

They could hardly wait.

Immediately, the states made their plans to switch places.

They said their good-byes, and went directly home to pack.

It took the better part of the next morning for the states to move to their new spots, but finally they were settled in. All of the states were much happier now that they were by their new neighbors and in a new part of the country. Oh yes, this was a much better arrangement!

But after a couple of days had passed and all the excitement had died down, the states began to realize that they weren't as happy as they thought.

Florida, who had switched spots with Minnesota, was FREEZING in the frosty northern climate. And Minnesota, who forgot to buy sunscreen, got an awful sunburn.

Alabama, New York, and Indiana—all of whom took California's place—were bothered by an annoying rumbling sound that kept them up all night.

Arizona, who had traded places with South Carolina, was upset because the ocean waves kept ruining her hairdo.

Alaska, who had been wanting a little more interaction with the other states, was irritated by Oklahoma's handle jabbing into his left side and Michigan's thumb tickling his right.

And worst of all, Kansas, who had switched places with Hawaii because he was sick of being stuck in the middle of the country, was now stuck in the middle of NOWHERE, feeling lonesome and seasick.

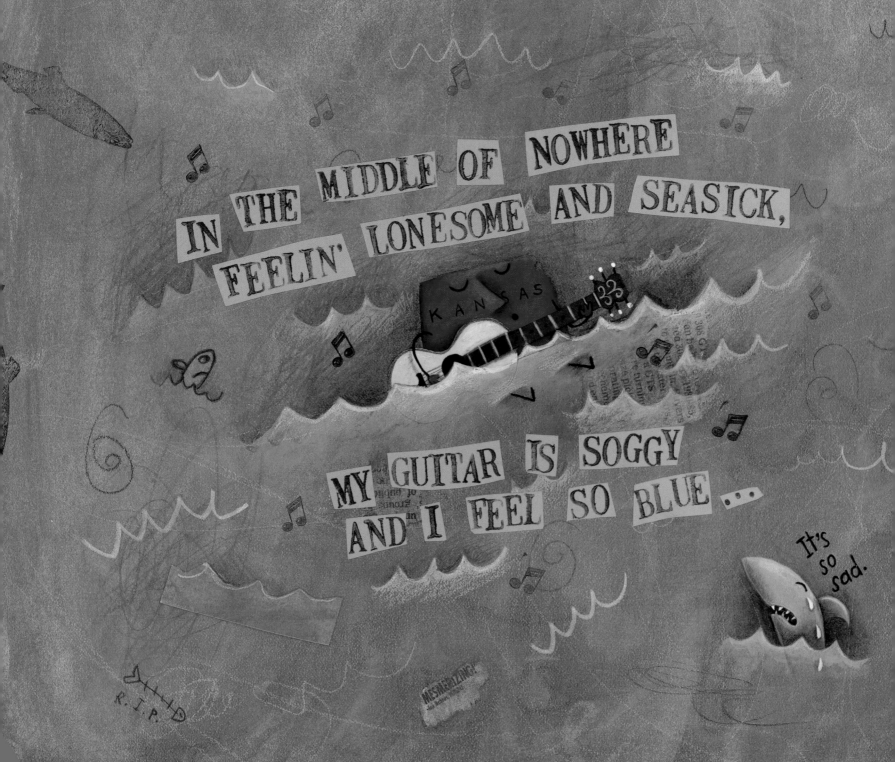

IN THE MIDDLE OF NOWHERE
FEELIN' LONESOME AND SEASICK,

MY GUITAR IS SOGGY
AND I FEEL SO BLUE ...

It's so sad.

R.I.P.

(And Hawaii was longing for some peace and quiet like in the good old days.)

Well, there was no question in any state's mind about what to do. Everyone wanted to go home! So, even faster than they made the first trip, they packed up their things and hit the road.

As the sun set across the country, all of the states—from A to W—were back in their very own homes. The states were so happy to see their old friends again. They spent the entire evening sharing their new experiences with each other—the good and the bad.

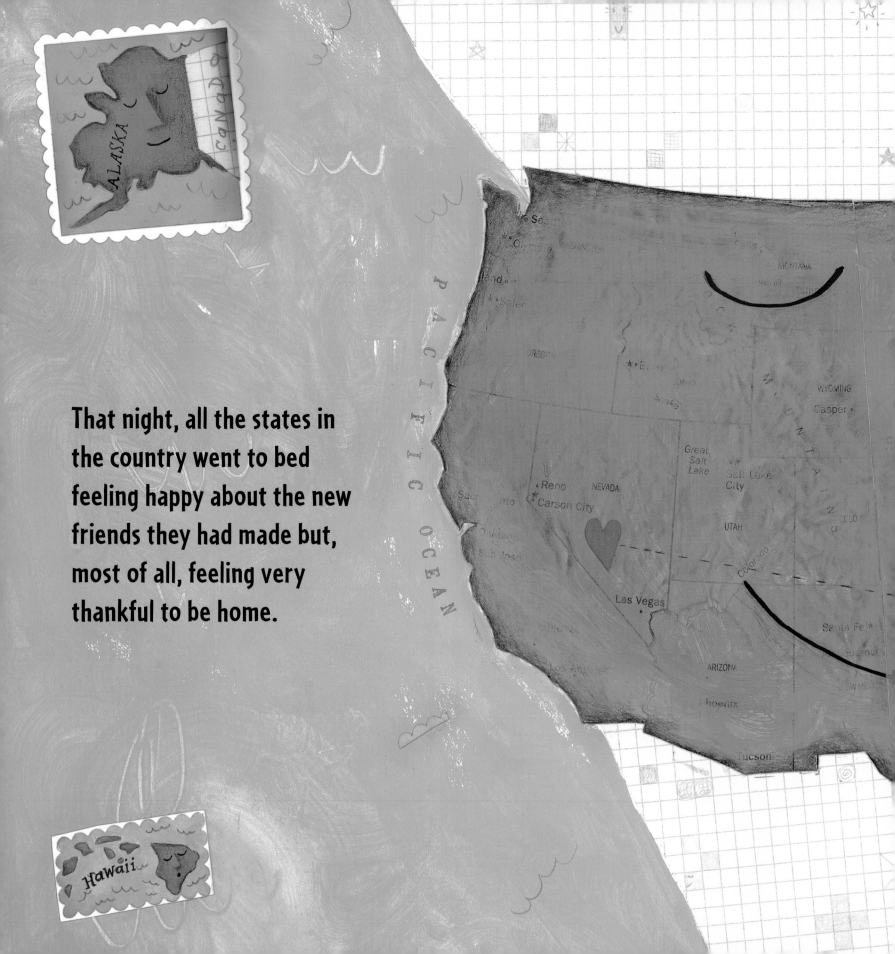

That night, all the states in the country went to bed feeling happy about the new friends they had made but, most of all, feeling very thankful to be home.

"Heart of Dixie"
ALABAMA

Capital: Montgomery
Square Miles: 50,767
Population: 4,083,000

"The Last Frontier"
ALASKA

Capital: Juneau
Square Miles: 570,830
Population: 525,000

"Grand Canyon State"
ARIZONA

Capital: Phoenix
Square Miles: 113,508
Population: 3,386,000

"Land of Opportunity"
ARKANSAS

Capital: Little Rock
Square Miles: 52,078
Population: 2,388,000

"Golden State"
CALIFORNIA

Capital: Sacramento
Square Miles: 156,299
Population: 27,663,000

"Centennial State"
COLORADO

Capital: Denver
Square Miles: 103,595
Population: 3,296,000

"Constitution State"
CONNECTICUT

Capital: Hartford
Square Miles: 4,872
Population: 3,211,000

"First State"
DELAWARE

Capital: Dover
Square Miles: 1,932
Population: 644,000

"Sunshine State"
FLORIDA

Capital: Tallahassee
Square Miles: 54,153
Population: 12,023,000

"Empire State of the South"
GEORGIA

Capital: Atlanta
Square Miles: 58,056
Population: 6,222,000

"Aloha State"
HAWAII

Capital: Honolulu
Square Miles: 6,425
Population: 1,083,000

"Gem State"
IDAHO

Capital: Boise
Square Miles: 82,412
Population: 998,000

"Prairie State"
ILLINOIS

Capital: Springfield
Square Miles: 55,645
Population: 11,582,000

"Hoosier State"
INDIANA

Capital: Indianapolis
Square Miles: 35,932
Population: 5,531,000

"Hawkeye State"
IOWA

Capital: Des Moines
Square Miles: 55,965
Population: 2,834,000

"Sunflower State"
KANSAS

Capital: Topeka
Square Miles: 81,778
Population: 2,476,000

"Bluegrass State"
KENTUCKY

Capital: Frankfort
Square Miles: 39,669
Population: 3,727,000

"Pelican State"
LOUISIANA

Capital: Baton Rouge
Square Miles: 44,521
Population: 4,461,000

"Pine Tree State"
MAINE

Capital: Augusta
Square Miles: 30,995
Population: 1,187,000

"Old Line State"
MARYLAND

Capital: Annapolis
Square Miles: 9,837
Population: 4,535,000

"Bay State"
MASSACHUSETTS

Capital: Boston
Square Miles: 7,824
Population: 5,855,000

"Great Lakes State"
MICHIGAN

Capital: Lansing
Square Miles: 56,594
Population: 9,200,000

"North Star State"
MINNESOTA

Capital: St. Paul
Square Miles: 79,548
Population: 4,246,000

"Magnolia State"
MISSISSIPPI

Capital: Jackson
Square Miles: 47,233
Population: 2,625,000

"Show Me State"
MISSOURI

Capital: Jefferson City
Square Miles: 68,945
Population: 5,103,000

"Treasure State"
MONTANA

Capital: Helena
Square Miles: 145,388
Population: 809,000

"Cornhusker State"
NEBRASKA

Capital: Lincoln
Square Miles: 76,644
Population: 1,594,000

"Sagebrush State"
NEVADA

Capital: Carson City
Square Miles: 109,894
Population: 1,007,000

"Granite State"
NEW HAMPSHIRE

Capital: Concord
Square Miles: 8,993
Population: 1,057,000

"Garden State"
NEW JERSEY

Capital: Trenton
Square Miles: 7,468
Population: 7,672,000

"Land of Enchantment"
NEW MEXICO

Capital: Santa Fe
Square Miles: 121,335
Population: 1,500,000

"Empire State"
NEW YORK

Capital: Albany
Square Miles: 47,377
Population: 17,825,000

"Tar Heel State"
NORTH CAROLINA

Capital: Raleigh
Square Miles: 48,843
Population: 6,413,000

"Peace Garden State"
NORTH DAKOTA

Capital: Bismarck
Square Miles: 69,300
Population: 672,000

"Buckeye State"
OHIO

Capital: Columbus
Square Miles: 41,004
Population: 10,784,000

"Sooner State"
OKLAHOMA

Capital: Oklahoma City
Square Miles: 68,655
Population: 3,272,000

"Beaver State"
OREGON

Capital: Salem
Square Miles: 96,184
Population: 2,724,000

"Keystone State"
PENNSYLVANIA

Capital: Harrisburg
Square Miles: 44,888
Population: 11,936,000

"Ocean State"
RHODE ISLAND

Capital: Providence
Square Miles: 1,055
Population: 947,154

"Palmetto State"
SOUTH CAROLINA

Capital: Columbia
Square Miles: 30,203
Population: 3,425,000

"Coyote State"
SOUTH DAKOTA

Capital: Pierre
Square Miles: 75,952
Population: 709,000

"Volunteer State"
TENNESSEE

Capital: Nashville
Square Miles: 41,155
Population: 4,855,000

"Lone Star State"
TEXAS

Capital: Austin
Square Miles: 262,017
Population: 16,789,000

"Beehive State"
UTAH

Capital: Salt Lake City
Square Miles: 82,073
Population: 1,680,000

"Green Mountain State"
VERMONT

Capital: Montpelier
Square Miles: 9,273
Population: 548,000

"Old Dominion"
VIRGINIA

Capital: Richmond
Square Miles: 39,704
Population: 5,904,000

"Evergreen State"
WASHINGTON

Capital: Olympia
Square Miles: 66,511
Population: 4,409,000

"Mountain State"
WEST VIRGINIA

Capital: Charleston
Square Miles: 24, 119
Population: 1,897,000

"Badger State"
WISCONSIN

Capital: Madison
Square Miles: 54,426
Population: 4,807,000

"Equality State"
WYOMING

Capital: Cheyenne
Square Miles: 96,989
Population: 509,000

CANADA

way
up
there

Alaska   canada

Washington   Montana   North Dakota

OREGON   Idaho   Wyoming   South Dakota   Minnesot

Pacific Ocean   Nebraska   IO

California   Nevada   Utah   Colorado   Kansas

Arizona   New Mexico   oklahoma

way
down
there
Hawaii

MEXICO   TEXAS

Michigan

Wisconsin

New York

Vermont
New Hampshire
Maine

Massachusetts

Rhode Island

Connecticut

Illinois

Indiana

Ohio

Pennsylvania

New Jersey

Delaware

Maryland

West Virginia

Virginia

Kentucky

North Carolina

Missouri

Tennessee

South Carolina

Arkansas

Mississippi

Alabama

GEORGIA

Atlantic Ocean

Louisiana

FLORIDA

LAURIE KELLER

is the author and illustrator of *The Scrambled States of America* and *Open Wide: Tooth School Inside*. A freelance artist who graduated from Kendall College of Art and Design, Laurie had always felt destined to write a book about the reorganization of the states. In first grade she rearranged her teacher's seating chart to best meet her needs. It was only a matter of time before she moved on to bigger things.

www.lauriekeller.com